# AS YOU WATCH OVER ME

written by
Julie Awerkamp & Holly Andreason

illustrated by
Jesi Yap

*For Benjamin, Grant, Zeke, and all the other little angels who are watching over us.*
*—Julie, Holly, & Jesi*

This edition first published in 2023
by Lawley Publishing,
a division of Lawley Enterprises LLC

Text copyright © 2023 Jolly Good Books
Illustration copyright © 2023 Jesi Yap
All Rights Reserved
Hardcover ISBN 978-1-960137-10-4
Paperback ISBN 978-1-960137-12-8
Library of Congress Control Number: 2023935600

Lawley Publishing
70 S. Val Vista Dr. #A3 #188
Gilbert, AZ 85296
LawleyPublishing.com

I can't believe the news I heard,
I wish it wasn't true.

You've gone away to heaven,

and I'm left missing you.

My family is emotional, but numb is all I feel.

My insides are so jumbled, I'm sure this can't be real.

I've never felt like this before.
I want to run away,
pretend it didn't happen,
ignore it for today.
But trying to avoid it all won't really bring relief.

I have to work through feelings,

a process known as

grief.

I'm learning as the days go by that grief has many sides.
Like water in the ocean, it comes and goes in tides.

At times I feel so sad inside and then I start to cry.
My tears will not stop falling, no matter what I try.

But then I'll go a day or two without you on my mind.

It leaves me feeling guilty, as if you're left behind.

I make a lot of promises that I'll be extra good,
if that will change what's happened.
I really wish it could.

When I can laugh or tell a joke and have a happy day,
I wonder if glad feelings are wrong in any way.

Some mornings I lay much too long
curled tightly up in bed.
I know I should get moving,
I'd rather sleep instead.

Yes, grief shows up in many ways, but I will not lose hope.
Throughout my hardest moments, there are good ways to cope.

I'm learning helpful strategies and practicing a few.

I can **write**

or **sing**

or **draw**.

A walk will help me too.

I'll take
**deep breaths**
and
**meditate**

or run and kick a ball.

I'll share our happy memories, put photos on my wall.

I'll give my family lots of hugs,
find comfort as I pray,

CONNECT with friends who LOVE me,

do something kind each day.

Some days ahead will still be hard no matter what I do.
I'll trust that all these feelings will help me make it through.

This grief won't leave me all at once, but I can start to see, that I'll find peace and healing

## AS YOU WATCH OVER ME.

Printed in the USA
CPSIA information can be obtained
at www.ICGtesting.com
CBHW041556181023
1388CB00024B/53